IN SEARCH OF A RIVER

Saroj Mukherjee is a well-known author of children's stories in Hindi. Her book *Anokha Aspatal* was made into an award-winning film and screened at the Frankfurt and Chicago Children's Film Festivals. Several English translations of her books have been published by reputed publishers like the Children's Book Trust and Mango Books. Orient BlackSwan has included sections of these translations in its children's schoolbooks and the original Hindi stories are also part of the vernacular school curriculum. Saroj Mukherjee has published several articles in renowned publications such as *The Telegraph*, *Dharmayug* and *Sarita*.

Born and educated in Allahabad (now Prayagraj), she lives in Kolkata. She is passionate about nature, the environment and wildlife, which is all reflected in the topics and contents of her stories.

Dr Tilottama Tharoor is the daughter of well-known writer Saroj Mukherjee and grew up in Kolkata. She currently teaches literature and the arts at New York University, USA. She shares a great love of stories with her mother, brother Dr Chandrashekhar Mukherji and two sons—Kanishk and Ishaan.

IN SEARCH OF A RIVER

Saroj Mukherjee

Translated from the Hindi original by
Tilottama Tharoor

Illustrations by
Trisha Dasgupta and Sreemoyee Ray

RUPA

Published by
Rupa Publications India Pvt. Ltd 2022
7/16, Ansari Road, Daryaganj
New Delhi 110002

Sales centres:
Allahabad Bengaluru Chennai
Hyderabad Jaipur Kathmandu
Kolkata Mumbai

Copyright © Saroj Mukherjee 2022

All rights reserved.

No part of this publication may be reproduced, transmitted,
or stored in a retrieval system, in any form or by any means,
electronic, mechanical, photocopying, recording or otherwise,
without the prior permission of the publisher.

This is a work of fiction. Names, characters, places and incidents are either the
product of the author's imagination or are used fictitiously and any resemblance
to any actual person, living or dead, events or locales is entirely coincidental.

ISBN: 978-93-5520-353-3

First impression 2022

10 9 8 7 6 5 4 3 2 1

The moral right of the author has been asserted.

This book is sold subject to the condition that it shall not, by way
of trade or otherwise, be lent, resold, hired out, or otherwise circulated,
without the publisher's prior consent, in any form of binding or
cover other than that in which it is published.

*For my great grandchildren
Eliseo, Ximena and Kahaani and
their fathers, after whom the central characters are named.*

One

My name is Bharat, but this story is not about me. This is a story based on events that took place long ago. It is about a wonderful adventure and a boy named Hanumant—a dear friend who stood by me whenever we faced unforeseen dangers. It was then that I understood that the history of a country cannot be known just by reading books.

Alongside the important events in a country, one should know something about the people living in it and their ways of life. Our nation is huge, with diverse people, including various tribes. To find out about them and respect their ways of life is to begin one's journey of understanding the true history of our land. Only then can we truly be proud and appreciate what we have.

Saroj Mukherjee

My father was an engineer. He used to travel to different parts of the country to supervise construction work. Because of this, he didn't stay in one place for too long. For this reason, I studied in a boarding school and came home only during the holidays. Sometimes, I even spent my holidays in places where I was all by myself, with no friends.

That summer, when I came home and saw my parents' place, I felt sure that this holiday too would be spent alone, reading books.

The town was small and our house was located at some distance from it. There was no way to get to the town via train since it was not connected to the railway network. I had taken a bus home with a friend of my father's. Ma and Papa came to the bus stop to receive me. My mother's happiness whenever I came home was the usual—it is what all children staying away from home are used to seeing and feeling. She started crying with joy. Papa said, seeing the tears, 'You are remarkable—you cry when he comes and also when he goes! Please smile a little!'

When we reached home, Papa asked about my studies.

Ma said, 'He has just come home! He has been studying all these days! Don't you see how thin he has become!'

Laughing and looking at me Papa said, 'He has become thin because he was without you! Now that he has come home and you have been preparing the dishes he likes—for

In Search of a River

the last one week—he will become healthy, just the way you want him!'

Ma was sitting near me. She kept touching me affectionately, as if she wanted to be certain that I was actually there. Papa laughed again and said, 'Pinch yourself and be sure that you are not dreaming.'

Ma, who had been smiling all this while, got up and said, 'There's no need to make fun of me. It's only natural I should miss him, and I know you do too, so don't pretend!'

Every time I returned from school, there was such happy and light-hearted talk, which gave me a warm feeling, reminding me that I was back home, and that nothing had changed! Our house had two storeys and the bedrooms were on the top floor. At the boarding school, I had to get up early every morning. Therefore, when I came home during my holidays, I got up late. Ma also encouraged me to sleep in.

However, the following day, I was woken up suddenly by loud voices from below. At first, I could not grasp where I was—home or some place else. It took some time for me to register where the voices were coming from. Someone was shouting.

I got out of bed and went to the window. When I looked out, I was amazed.

Next to the house was a garden. A tall man with a big moustache was trying to chase a boy out of the garden,

In Search of a River

threatening him with a stick. The boy was sitting high up on the branch of a tree and laughing at the man.

'You monkey, why do you come every day and jump around? Run away, otherwise you will feel this stick on your back!' the man shouted, waving the stick.

'You have to say my name aloud first! What is my name? Just say it once,' the boy demanded, laughing.

'I will tell you your name—monkey! Now shall I hit you with my stick?'

'My name is not "monkey". Tell me my real name, Misir Kaka!"

It was really a funny scene. The boy was laughing, sitting on the branch, and Misir Kaka, with a stick in his hand, was jumping around in anger!

Ma must have heard the shouting and, thinking that it may have woken me up, she came upstairs. She came up to me at the window and said, 'This happens every morning. Misir ji sure does a lot of jumping around!'

'Who is this Misir ji?' I asked.

'The owner of this house has a small garden next door. Misir ji looks after the garden. He has another name, but everyone calls him Misir Kaka,' Ma said, smiling.

'Who is the boy?' I asked.

'There is a village nearby where some tribal communities live. He is the son of Bisu Sardar, the village headman. Most probably, he studies in the school in town. This is holiday time, so he comes every day and runs around in the garden,' said Ma who couldn't stop laughing. It seemed like she also enjoyed watching the antics of Misir Kaka and the boy. This shouting and dancing around every day obviously pleased her to no end.

'Has Papa left for work?' I asked.

'Yes, quite some time ago. Now wash and come down for breakfast,' said Ma while leaving the room.

After breakfast, I decided to look around our house and explore the area. Ma, as always, urged me to be careful, saying, 'Bharat, don't go too far, this is an unknown place. There are lots of poisonous insects here.'

It seems that every mother finds some danger lurking around her children. I had seen how my grandmother would also ask Papa to be careful. I had asked him once, 'Now you are grown up, don't you find this upsetting?'

'No, Bharat, I like it,' he had said. 'There is someone who still thinks I am little and worries about me.'

The garden next to our house had many big trees. Misir Kaka was sitting on a small cot under a tree. Upon seeing me wandering in the garden, he called out to me, saying, 'Bhaiya, come here.' I folded my hands in namaskar, in return.

'Bhabhi ji had told me that you would be coming. She has been looking forward to having you home.' He made

In Search of a River

me sit next to him on the cot.

'Do you look after this garden? And do you live here?' I asked.

'Yes, bhaiya. I have been here for a long time. This garden has become my home now,' he said.

'Whom were you shouting at in the morning?' I asked, a little fearful of being hit with the stick propped next to him. He was a very big man with a heavy moustache.

'Don't ask! Since his school has closed that monkey has been coming here and mucking around. Look, he has destroyed these plants by jumping on them!' he said loudly, but a smile had appeared on his face simultaneously.

'Is his name "Monkey"?' I asked.

This time, Misir ji answered after a pause. 'He has another name. But I call him Bandar, Monkey,' he said slowly. I sensed he was reluctant to speak further, so I kept quiet.

In the evening when Papa came home, I asked him, 'Who are these tribals?'

'Who are you asking about?' He looked at me with surprise.

'I saw a boy in the morning. He had a bird's feather tied on his head, with a red ribbon and a string of multicoloured beads. He carried a bow and arrow. He was dressed up as if he was going on stage or to act in a play. Misir ji said his name is Bandar.'

Papa smiled broadly and said, 'So you have seen the first act of the morning drama! He is the son of Bisu Sardar and his name is Hanumant, not Bandar or Monkey.'

'Then why did Misir ji call him Bandar?' I asked.

'You better ask Misir ji for an answer. He is the only one who can give you the correct answer,' Papa replied, laughing and looking at Ma. This was how the first day of my holiday passed. In the evening, we sat down and talked about all that had happened during the time I was away.

I asked Papa whether the people working with him were from tribal communities and wanted to know who they were exactly.

'Yes, the people who live in the village nearby are Adivasis, original tribes who have been living here since ancient times. They are working with us. You must come with me and see the work going on. We are making a bridge. This is going to be a very large bridge. During the rainy season, the river becomes very wide. Without a proper bridge, the people living hereabouts have great difficulty crossing the river,' he explained.

We were up talking till late at night, until I began to feel sleepy and went to bed.

Two

The next day, the same drama unfolded. This time, I took a good look at the boy sitting on the tree branch. He was almost my age—or he may have been younger, eleven or twelve years old—and seemed shorter than I was. He wore a white dhoti and his upper body was bare, with only a string of coloured beads around his neck.

After breakfast, I went up to Misir ji. He was working in the garden. Upon seeing me he said, 'Bharat bhaiya, come and sit near me.' He then greeted me with folded hands, raising them a little to ensure they touched his head.

'Can I ask you something,' I said, hesitatingly.

'Yes ... yes ... Ask.'

'This morning that boy had come again. Why don't you tell me his name?' I asked him.

This time he looked a little upset—as if he didn't know what to say.

'My father said his name is Hanumant,' I said.

'Yes, that is his name. But I perform the Hanumant Mahabir puja every day. Now you tell me, how can I do my puja and then chase him, calling him by the same name? That is why I call him monkey—doesn't he look like a bandar?'

I started chuckling, and soon both of us were laughing together.

Having seen and heard all this, I wanted to meet Hanumant. If we could become friends then I would have a companion during these holidays. I asked Misir Kaka, 'Where will he be at this time?'

'Who knows where he will be now! When the school is closed, he wears feathers on his head and roams about in the hills and the forest. His father, Bisu Sardar, works with the bridge workers and goes to the construction site, so the monkey is totally free.'

I realized that it was not possible to get any information out of Misir Kaka, so I thought I would look for Hanumant on my own.

I went home and told Ma, 'I am going to explore the area.' I thought that if I mentioned Hanumant's name she would start worrying.

'Where will you go? It is a forest all around—'

In Search of a River

'—There might be snakes and other animals!' I added and we both started laughing. 'Don't worry, I will be nearby and if you call me, I'll come,' I said, hoping that it was enough to keep her from worrying too much.

There were no small trees and plants near our house, but many small hillocks. The town was near the hills. There was a big river on the other side of the town where the railway bridge was being built. After passing Misir Kaka's garden, I started walking further through the big, tall trees. There seemed to be a village beyond the trees. I had not walked far when suddenly, an arrow flew down from above and landed on the ground, right in front of me.

Startled, I stepped back, and then a voice from above commanded me saying, 'Don't move! This land is mine!'

I looked up and saw the same boy sitting on a tree branch. I was surprised, and a little angry. Looking up at him, I said, 'Who are you and why are you stopping me from going ahead?'

He climbed down to a lower branch and then jumped down. Facing me, he said, 'Tell me who *you* are! It seems like you are a newcomer and don't know me! Tell me who you are first, only then will I tell you who I am.'

'You tell me—what would have happened if this arrow had hit me?' I replied.

He chuckled and said, 'An arrow by Hanumant only hits

In Search of a River

his target and nothing else. I had aimed at a nishana, and it went there, and nowhere else!'

I was astonished. He was so young and yet such a great nishaneybaaz. But hiding my surprise, I said, 'Hitting someone with an arrow without warning is not correct.'

He seemed astonished at my remark. He looked at me from head to toe, as though examining me to check if I was hurt. In the meantime, I thought, 'If I want for us to be friends, why should I quarrel with him?'

And so I extended my hand and said, 'My name is Bharat. I think your name is Hanumant, is it not? I have seen you jumping around the trees in Misir Kaka's garden. He is right—you do look like a monkey,' I said, smiling.

Hearing Misir Kaka's name, he started laughing. He took my hand and said, 'Bharat and Hanumant! We're old friends.'

This was true. I had not thought about this coincidence. In the epic Ramayana, the two were indeed friends!

We started walking together. After we emerged from under the trees he pointed and said, 'That side—across the nala—is our village. We stay there.'

I saw a riverbed near the hill, with hardly any water in it, mostly stones. 'Is there no water in this nala?' I asked.

'The water dries up in summer. But when it rains, the water from the falls across the hill fills the nala,' he said.

'Then how do you cross the nala without a bridge?'

'By jumping on the stones,' he said, laughing. 'My name is Hanumant, and jumping and climbing is what I do. Hasn't Misir Kaka told you?'

'You may jump across, but what do the other villagers do?'

'They build a narrow bamboo bridge. Only people cross the bridge—no cars or trucks.' After this, he was quiet for some time, as if he was thinking about something. Then he said, 'When I grow up, I will become an engineer like your father and my first job will be to build a bridge—a bridge people will come to see from far and wide.'

Looking at him, I felt as if he could see this bridge that he had just imagined.

'Will you take me to your village?' I asked.

'Will you come to my home? My Baba—grandfather, my father's father, we call him Baba—can tell you many stories. He knows a lot about this area and our people.'

'Who else lives with you in your home?' I asked.

'My father, my mother, a small brother and a sister. My father works with the bridge builders across the city. Ma stays at home. She makes very beautiful clay toys. We decorate our home with these toys.'

Hearing him talking about his village and home, I could tell that he was very proud and fond of them. 'I would love to come to your village and meet your mother, Baba and

In Search of a River

your brother and sister. When will you take me? Your father knows my father.'

'Come now!'

He seemed very keen to take me with him.

'It has gotten late now. I have not told Ma, and if I am late in returning home, she will get worried. Tomorrow I will come with you to your home after I have told Ma and Papa about it,' I promised.

We lingered, wandering around for a while. I asked, 'Who taught you archery?'

'I learnt it from my father, and he learnt it from his father. We learn it in our early years, when we are small.'

'Can you teach me?'

'Why not? But you have to practise every day. My father says it's only when your mind and eyes focus on a target that your aim is accurate and perfect.'

It was getting late so I returned home. I did not tell anyone about my meeting with Hanumant, or about our new friendship and my desire to learn archery. Ma would worry. But perhaps, my father would support me and agree to all this.

Three

My worst fears had come to life. When I told Papa and Ma that I would like to go to Hanumant's village, and learn how to use a bow and arrow, they were concerned. Ma, who was very upset, said, 'You have come home after such a long time. Instead of resting and being here with me, you decide on this madness! The village of the tribals is a wild place—there are hills, jungles and other dangerous spots. We don't know those people, or what and who they are! No, you will not go to the village.'

Hoping Papa would be able to do something, I turned towards him. He smiled and said, 'Kamla, your son cannot sit at home all through his holiday. You are worried about those people, but I know Bisu Sardar very well. We know Hanumant too and he is Bharat's age. If they stay together,

In Search of a River

Bharat will be happy. I know that will please you.'

'How does it matter to you?' Ma argued. 'You will be away at work. It will be me who will worry all the time.'

'What is there to worry about?' Papa was trying to calm her down.

'He said that he wants to learn how to shoot arrows. What will happen if he gets hit and wounded?'

'Oh God, you have imagined all kinds of injuries. They will not be playing with arrows like Ram and Ravan, trying to kill each other!' Papa put a hand on Ma's back, trying to soothe her. 'Kamla, these people belong here, to an old tribe. They've lived here for a long time. They know all the places around here. They know how to look after themselves. They will also look after us. I will speak to Bisu Sardar about Bharat. Don't worry!'

Ma fell silent but she was not happy about the situation— one look at her and the message would be loud and clear. Papa turned to me and said, 'Bharat, you are growing up. You are no longer a child. After some time, you will have to look after us. You should not do anything that might make your mother worried and unhappy. If you're careful, then you will be safe and we needn't worry.'

I nodded in agreement. Papa had helped me, I understood, but he had also made me aware of my responsibilities.

After breakfast the next morning, I got ready to leave.

Ma filled a flask with cold sherbet and gave it to me saying I should only drink this and avoid water anywhere else.

Seeing her worried face, I said lovingly, 'I will be careful. Please don't worry at all.'

I had already seen Hanumant was waiting for me from the window; he was sitting on the compound wall. As he saw me coming, he jumped down with such agility that I laughed aloud.

He was surprised and asked me, 'What happened?'

'Misir Kaka was right,' I replied. 'If a tail is attached to you, you will become a monkey.'

He grinned and then pointed to my flask to say, 'What is in that?'

'Sherbet. When we feel thirsty, we will both drink it. Ma has forbidden me to drink water from anywhere else,' I told him.

'Why?'

'There are germs in dirty water. They can make us fall ill. Haven't you read this in your schoolbooks?' I asked with curiosity.

'Oh, we are told many things in school, but they are not of any use to us. My father says that we should follow nature and its rules. Nature helps us. This has also been told to us by our tribal leaders,' he replied.

'Old knowledge is good,' I agreed, 'but my Papa says

In Search of a River

that when we have access to new scientific proofs and its advantages, then it is not always right to follow ideas without proof. You study in school too, which class are you studying in?' I had not asked about his school before, even though he had become my friend.

'I am in the sixth standard, and you?' he asked.

'I am in seventh—one year senior to you. You must show respect,' I said with a grin.

'Well, you may be one year ahead of me in school, but I am senior to you in the bow and arrow class,' he replied, 'so, we are even.'

Hanumant seemed like someone who would never acknowledge himself to be anything other than an equal when compared to someone else. Soon, we were laughing and joking with great ease. After some time, we were to cross the small river.

'Is this where you hope to make a big bridge? But there is no water in this riverbed. Where will the bridge be made?' I asked, genuinely puzzled.

He replied without hesitation. 'You will see the bridge I'll make here. It will be a beautiful bridge. My grandfather says that there used to be a river, which was once full of water. Why it dried up, no one knows. Now water fills it up only when it rains. When I grow up, I will find out why this river dried up. Can you see the hill? The water used to

In Search of a River

come from under it. My grandfather says that the river got angry and went underground.'

'Great! This is the first time I've heard that a river gets angry and goes away,' I said, surprised at the revelation. A very slender line of water was flowing between the stones. We crossed it by stepping on the stones and reached the other side.

We could see a little village up ahead, with small huts made of mud. As we neared those huts, I saw that the mud walls were decorated with beautiful images of birds and animals. The huts looked very clean. Hanumant pointed towards one and said it was his home.

An old man was sitting in front of the hut and near him sat a woman who was wearing a white sari and seemed busy at work. Hanumant told me that this was his grandfather, and that the lady sitting near him was his mother. He said, 'My grandfather and my mother only speak our tribal language. You will not be able to understand it.'

'But you speak like us,' I said.

'I study and go to school, where I learn your language. Before going to school, I too couldn't speak or understand it. They—he pointed to his family—have not been to school.'

'Don't worry,' I said, 'you can be our translator and explain what we don't understand.'

Now while narrating this story, I have tried to convey

what was said as accurately as possible. After all, when you read this, Hanumant may not be nearby to translate it for you.

We had reached Hanumant's house. His mother, who was making something with wet mud, had seen us. She was moulding the mud swiftly and expertly. It looked like a bird to me. When she saw me looking, she said, 'Sugga.'

I turned to Hanumant for help.

He told me that she was making a clay parrot. 'After being painted, it will look exactly like a parrot. Ma makes these toys and sells them in the market.'

I smiled and looked at Hanumant's mother. She had turned her attention towards us and was smiling as well. She seemed to understand what he'd said, because she nodded. I looked at her. Her hair was black and was tied behind in a bun with a red flower tucked into it. She looked beautiful. Hanumant told his Baba in his own language or bhasha that I was the son of 'Engineer Babu', my name was Bharat and that I was Hanumant's friend. Baba lifted his hands and expressed his joy. Hanumant had told me before that his grandfather could not see properly. But both of them seemed glad to have us around and were very welcoming of me. His mother got up, went inside and brought out some puffed rice in two small bowls with chana and gur. She put it in front of me and gestured that I should eat it. When I finished eating, she sat near me. Really, I will never forget that

In Search of a River

chana–gur. It was delicious. Whenever I think of Hanumant, I also remember his Baba and Ma. These are memories that will always be with me.

Then, it was time for my archery lesson. I soon realized that it is not at all easy to master the skill. You must have seen a bow and arrow. I had thought that just by placing the arrow in the middle and pulling the string, the arrow would fly straight and hit the target, but alas, something else happened. First, the arrow hardly left the bow and simply landed near my feet. The second time, it went behind me. In frustration, I turned towards Hanumant who could barely hide his amusement.

'Why are you standing there and smiling? Please help me,' I said, feeling cross. We had climbed a hill for the bow and arrow practice.

'Let me show you again,' he offered patiently. He aimed his arrow at a point he had marked earlier and it swiftly pierced it. I couldn't believe how easy he made it look, but when my chance came again, it was as if the arrow had ideas of its own! Instead of going straight, it wanted to go to the right or left, or even behind me—not in front. Seeing my repeated failures, Hanumant began to feel sorry for me. He put his hand on mine, making the grip firmer. This time, the arrow did not hit the mark, but it went near enough.

Hanumant was pleased. 'You will soon learn by practising

like this,' he assured me. 'Only look at the mark you plan to hit and not anywhere else.' He spoke with the authority of a teacher, and I listened obediently, like a student.

In the days that followed, shooting arrows was not our only activity. After our short practice session, Hanumant would take me wandering, venturing into the hills near our home and surrounding places. I could tell from the way Hanumant would explore the countryside that he was searching for something. Most probably, the lost river near the hills.

Four

Thinking of the dried-up river near the hill that once used to be full of water and remembering how Hanumant's grandfather had said that for some reason the river had become angry and gone underground, I suggested that Hanumant and I should go up the hill to look around. I found this story of the angry river very intriguing.

We started the next day. It would take us about one hour to reach the hill. It was not very high and we hoped we could climb it with ease. I asked him, 'Have you ever gone to the top of the hill?'

'Many times,' he said. 'There was a king's palace at the top. Now, only a few broken walls are left.'

'Where has the king gone?'

'Where would they go? All of them died fighting each

other. Baba says that two of his sons fought to become the king and both died.'

This time, we had taken some food with us. I had somehow managed to convince Ma to accept our plan of spending the whole day exploring the hills until evening. Papa had spoken to Bisu Sardar who had told him not to worry. 'Hanumant knows the surroundings and the people living in the village will also look after Bharat.'

We started climbing the hill. A rough trail, trees and stones helped us in our climb. It was beautiful when we reached the top. We could see the dry riverbed and the village with its dollhouses from this height.

'Does no one stay here?' I asked.

'No. This is known as the hill of the king. It is said that no one should spend the night here. The villagers leave before it gets dark!'

'What are they afraid of? Are there ghosts here?'

'Baba says that the king's treasure is buried here. It is guarded by the snake god. Seeing anyone near this place angers the snakes.'

I didn't really believe what he said, but I still had to caution him. 'Look, Hanumant, don't say this in front of my mother. Otherwise, she'll stop me from going out with you.'

He understood my concern, nodded and smiled.

Two or three walls were all that was left of the king's

In Search of a River

palace, all of which was broken. How old was the palace? One could not tell. At one time, it would have been full of people and activity, but today it was a lonely, deserted ruin in a jungle.

After the climb, both of us were feeling tired and hungry. We shared the sandwiches I had brought and the gur, chivda and chana he had got for the day. I ended up eating most of the food he had brought. He looked at the sandwiches made by my mother and then asked, 'What's in them?'

'Elephants and horses! Eat, try it!'

'I'm not afraid of eating an elephant or a horse!' he replied.

'Try it. There is chicken in it,' I urged, but by this time he had already bitten into one, along with a green chilli he had brought with him. He seemed to like the combination very much, because he ate four or five and then said, 'I will tell you something, but first promise you will not tell anyone.'

'Papa says that one should not promise anything without first knowing what it's about,' I replied.

'No, it is nothing bad. If you don't like it, don't think about it, but don't tell anyone.'

'Well … I promise. I will not tell anyone!' I said, curious to know what he wanted to tell me.

'There is a nag here. I have seen it!'

'Nag? You mean a snake?' Then I remembered. 'You said that the king's treasure is buried here and a snake king looks

In Search of a River

after it—the *same* nag?'

'Treasure is what they say, but I have seen the nag ... and he is my friend!' he said and stared, as if to check if I believed him.

'A snake is your friend? You are a wonderful person—you are like a monkey and you make friends with a snake!'

I actually couldn't believe him and thought it was all a joke.

'No,' he insisted. 'What I am saying is true. He sees me and never harms me. When I come here, I bring some milk for him and pour it out for him to drink.' Saying this, he brought out a small bottle from a cloth tied around his waist, with milk in it. 'Bharat, I'm going to the other side of the old broken wall. You can come with me—I will then go alone to the other side, as the nag lives there. He does not know you, so you should only see him from far.'

'He will not bite you?'

Now I was getting scared. Hanumant was clever, but he was also reckless. Who knew what might happen. And the snake made me fearful.

Hanumant was already headed towards the broken wall, and I followed. I was not going to stay behind alone. He stopped near the wall, turned towards me, signalling for me to stay there, and then started advancing further.

The old walls of the broken palace were in front of us,

and the surrounding area was scattered with crumbling stones that had plants growing out of them. Hanumant, after crossing the broken walls, placed the milk in a mud cup and put it under a tree. He pursed his lips and made a sound like a whistle. After some time, from between the two stones, a snake slowly slithered out. It was black and quite long.

It came straight towards Hanumant, stopped in front of him, raised itself and spread its hood wide, swaying slightly. I would have run away in fear if my feet had not felt like they were stuck to the ground. I just stood there, transfixed, and I watched. Hanumant started talking to him, shaking his head. What he was saying, I could not hear, but I saw the snake bring his head closer. After some time, Hanumant folded his hands, offered a namaskar and gradually stepped away.

I too wanted to retreat, but my legs started to shake. I managed to go back a few steps, and found a stone to sit on.

Hanumant stood there, watching the snake for a while and then he came towards me.

'What's the matter, Bharat? Don't be afraid—that nag will not harm you. Now let us go down,' he said, holding my arm as he helped me up.

We walked along for some time quietly. After a while, I asked, 'How did you become friends with this snake?'

'One day I had come to the top of this hill and was wandering around. Suddenly, it came out and stood before

In Search of a River

me with its head held high. I am telling you, truly, I was very scared, but I stood quietly before him. Baba says that a nag never attacks anyone for no reason. Our tribe has been living near this jungle for a long time. We worship the nag. It is said that the nag knows what you are thinking. It looked at me for some time and then went away quietly, and since then, my fear has also gone.'

We were going down the hill when suddenly Hanumant picked up something from the ground. Showing it to me, he said with surprise, 'A half-burnt cigarette! Who around here smokes a cigarette? The village people smoke bidis. No one comes here from the city. This village is quite far for most people.'

I was not as surprised by it as he was. I still kept thinking of the snake with its raised hood. Reaching the bottom of the hill, I said, 'We should return home now, it will become dark very soon. Ma must be getting worried, and my heart is still thumping after meeting your "nag devata". Tomorrow morning, we will meet again. And tomorrow, I'd like to hear the story of the king from your Baba.'

'All right, I will tell Baba that you'll come tomorrow. He will be very happy. Whenever someone comes and talks to him, he enjoys it very much,' Hanumant said.

Both of us returned to our homes. That night, I could not sleep for a long time. Lying awake in bed, I kept returning to all that had happened in the morning. I once again felt the fear, but also the amazement. Hanumant had walked so close to a large snake, and he had made it drink milk brought by him and talked to it. It was astounding. If I had not seen it for myself, I would not have believed it.

Five

Hanumant said that his grandfather's doctor was planning to operate on one eye this winter, and then his Baba would have to wear spectacles. Talking to him was interesting, though understanding his language was difficult. Hanumant would often help and translate some of his words.

That day, when we went to him, he was sitting in front of his house and smoking a hukka. When I said 'Namaste Baba', he looked pleased and gestured for me to sit near him Then he called Hanumant's mother and asked her to bring me something to eat. I had noticed that the people of this area are very particular about welcoming and looking after their guests. His behaviour with me was, as always, full of affection.

When I asked him about the hill of the king he smiled and asked me if Hanumant had taken me there. 'He roams about the whole day, never sits down to study. Once his school closes, his roaming starts.'

'My school is also closed and my studies have also stopped,' I said with a lot of pleasure. 'Holidays are meant for wandering around. Please tell us the story of the tribal kings,' I pleaded.

He thought for some time and said, 'It is a very old story. I was not even born then. I had heard from my father that the king of our tribe used to live on top of the hill. People living in the villages around here respected him as their king, and he also looked after all of us. My father said that the king had two sons. They were not friendly with each other and would fight all the time. Their fighting made the king very unhappy.'

'Did the elder son become the king after him?' I asked.

'No, this is not the rule in our tribe. The leaders of the tribe decide who will become the king. This time, the king called the leaders and asked them what he could do as both his sons were fit to become king after him. None of the leaders could decide between them and the sons went on fighting.'

'What happened in the end?'

'Something very strange happened. One day, the king called everyone and said that he had had a dream in which

In Search of a River

he had seen the snake king; and he said, "I am going to take the throne and crown and I will hide them. Whoever is able to find them will be made the king." Hearing this, all the people became very scared and started to run in panic. The king's throne was made of stone and was quite heavy. The crown was made of silver and had coloured stones set in it. But both the items had disappeared and no one could find them.'

Baba paused, and I asked in surprise, 'Had the snake king really taken them away?'

'Who knows? But no one ever saw them again. When the king died, both his sons fought. One of them died and the other one, who wanted to be king, was not accepted by the leaders. Everyone searched for the throne and crown, but could not find them. Soon after, the river near our village also dried up. Everyone believed that this was because of the anger of the snake god. They said that until the throne and crown were found, the river would remain dry.'

'How did the river dry up?' I prodded him.

'This is a mountain river. They say the river became angry and went underground. Who knows what is true. But the people of our tribe do have great respect for the snake god.'

The story ended, but for me there were new mysteries. What happened to the throne and the crown? How did the river go underground? Do rivers go underground at all?

In Search of a River

Puzzled by these questions, Hanumant and I came to the bank of the dry river. Suddenly, I asked, 'Do you really think that the throne and crown were taken away by the snake god?'

Hanumant was upset on hearing my question. I wondered: as he belonged to the tribe, maybe he had faith in the snake god?

He spoke slowly. 'I have also thought about it many times: if there was a crown and a throne, where did they go?'

'I think the king himself hid them somewhere, and told everyone a made-up story about his dream and the snake god so that his sons and the leaders would believe that this was all done by the snake god,' I replied, after some thought.

'Why would he do that?'

'He probably did not want either of his sons to become king. He didn't think they were fit to become king after him.'

'You could be right.'

Hanumant was briefly silent after that, thinking about the new possibilities. 'Then the throne and the crown are somewhere here!' he suddenly said with excitement. 'Why don't we look for them?'

'If you look for them and find them then you will become king,' I said jokingly, pleased by his excitement.

'I don't want to become king,' he said, seriously, 'I have told you before, I want to be like your father and become an engineer. I have to build a bridge on the river.'

'Then we have to search for the river that has gone underground. Otherwise, your bridge will be made on a river without any water; an unusual bridge … yes?' I said, and my words made him laugh.

At home while having dinner, I asked Papa, 'Does a river ever go underground?'

Papa looked at me with surprise in his eyes.

'Hanumant's Baba was telling us that the dry river near his village used to be full of water earlier. Then it got angry and went underground,' I told him.

Hearing this, Papa started laughing. I had told him earlier about Hanumant's wish to become an engineer.

He asked, 'Is that where Hanumant's bridge will be built?'

'Yes! But is it true that there could have been a big river, which then became angry and went underground?'

'Bharat, I cannot say whether it happens because of anger or pleasure, but sometimes rivers are found flowing under mountains and they go underground for quite some distance, and then, they come up to the surface by themselves. This is a wonder of nature. Sometimes, a river flowing at the top of a mountain makes a hole and starts to drop inside the mountain—much like a waterfall. Then it may pour out of the mountain wherever there is a hole,' he said, making it easy for me to understand.

In Search of a River

'Have you seen a river like that?' I asked him curiously.

'Yes, I have seen a river flowing inside a mountain and a waterfall inside a mountain, both in Switzerland. But I did not ask the people there if this happened because the rivers were angry with us.' He smiled.

Ma, who was listening to us, said, 'You keep telling him all these unbelievable stories and getting him upset! As it is he spends the whole day wandering through the jungle—now he will start looking around for rivers that have gone underground.'

'Kamla, what I am saying is true. These are real wonders of nature. Knowing about them is increasing his knowledge. If your son finds a river that has gone underground, then it will be a great discovery. Rashtrapati ji will give him an award for it,' Papa said, still smiling.

Ma wasn't impressed. 'Please don't give him these ideas. As it is I keep worrying about him all day,' she repeated.

I was fascinated by what Papa said about the wonders of nature. I asked him to tell me more about them.

'Bharat, nature has many wonders and all of them are different and marvellous. We can't see them because we have no time to look around us. Even today when I think of the mountain in Switzerland and what I saw inside it, I am amazed. One stream of water did not fall like a waterfall, but emerged out of the mountain, like a river. The river was going through the inner stones and made its own way to come out of the mountain. People built steps to get inside the mountain and see all of it. If I had not seen it, I could have not imagined it.'

'You saw the river inside? Did you go in?' I asked Papa.

'Yes, I asked people who had been inside, because where we were standing, there were fields, houses and many fruit trees.'

'Where was the river?' I asked.

'At first, I couldn't see the river from where we were standing. "You are standing on top of the river," one of them smiled and told me. We looked at our feet with fear, thinking briefly if it is truly under us we may fall in.' Papa started laughing when he told me this.

'Then, we were taken to the opening of a cave, which looked like a small door, and we saw the river flowing inside! There were two or three boats, also inside. If someone wanted to go in and sail along the river, the boats took them into the mountain. "Where does the river go from here?" we asked. And were told, "Who knows, it may be flowing underneath till it comes out and joins another river further away." I have to say, Switzerland is a beautiful country, all mountains covered with snow and many lakes,' Papa said.

I was listening with full concentration to what Papa was saying. I wished I had seen all that too. 'Papa, do we have

In Search of a River

such places in our country?' I asked.

'Of course, we have many! Ours is a big country ... so finding them is not easy. We don't look after such places properly either, unlike other countries. There are wonderful places in the Himalayas. On one side, we have mountains covered with snow and, next to them, there are ponds with hot springs. When you grow up, you will be able to see these wonderful places in your own country,' he replied.

That night, I saw a gleaming river inside a mountain and a gushing waterfall ... in my dreams.

Six

I could not forget Hanumant's snake friend nor could I tell Papa or Ma about him. If Ma got to know about the snake, she would make me a prisoner in the house.

The next day, Hanumant and I decided not to go towards the hill, but go to the other side of the city, where they were making the big bridge. I asked Papa if we could go there.

'Why? What do you want to see there?' Ma asked when she heard this. 'Hanumant can become whatever he wants to—but I will not let you become a bridge-making engineer. I have had to wander around jungles and mountains all these years because of your father. If it is the same with the son then my old age will be miserable.'

Papa and I both couldn't help but laugh at Ma's complaints.

In Search of a River

When Hanumant and I arrived at the bridge, we saw many people working there. We decided to go down and sit near the river. There was not much water there either, but the riverbed was quite broad.

During the rains, it became quite dangerous, everyone said. When it flooded, it washed away most of what lay on its path. The bridge was being made for trains and cars, because a rail line was necessary to be able to reach this place. The old bridge had become unsafe for buses.

Hanumant quietly watched the work going on for some time, then he asked suddenly, 'How long does one have to study to become an engineer? Will it take many years?'

'One has to study a lot...' I said rather vaguely.

'After finishing school, what will I have to do?' Hanumant persisted.

'You will have to go to an engineering college for four or five years,' I said, trying to make him aware of the long road ahead. I remembered that Papa had mentioned it on a few occasions earlier.

Hanumant looked worried upon hearing this and said, 'Baba will become very old by then.'

'It won't be a problem—he will be able to see your bridge because he'll be wearing spectacles!' Suddenly, I remembered something and asked him, 'Please tell me, why were you named Hanumant by Baba? You said that you would tell me.'

My question made him smile. 'It's a very funny story. They were holding a Ramlila performance in the town. A drama company had come from another city. Some of the villagers went to see it. They had made a stage on the maidan and the audience was sitting on the ground. There was a tree near the stage, and a branch of the tree reached out and touched the corner of the stage. My Baba arrived late and sat near the stage, under the tree. The Ramlila was going on, and Sita ji was sitting on the stage, as though she was in the garden of Ashok Vatika.'

'Under the same tree?' I asked.

'No ... she was on the stage. The play was going on. Then Ravan came, and he shouted at her, trying to frighten her and he went away, still shouting. Sita ji was upset and frightened and started crying. Hanuman ji, who was sitting on the branch of the tree, dropped a ring near her. Seeing the ring, she picked it up and said, "Who has brought this?" Hanumant said this part as if he was acting in the play. 'Hearing her, the man who was dressed as Hanuman jumped down from the tree and said, "I am Ramsevak Hanuman, Mata ji." But his jump went a little wrong and he fell on my Baba, who was also under the tree. Baba was hurt, but the other people who were watching the Ramlila started laughing.'

We were also laughing by now.

'But how does this scene connect with your birth?' I asked.

In Search of a River

'Baba had to be helped home by some people. He reached home just after I was born. Hearing about my birth he said, "Today Hanuman ji fell on my head and he has come to my home too." That is why I was named Hanumant.'

In the meantime, work on the bridge was proceeding quite fast. Papa had said that the work underwater should be completed before the start of the rains, otherwise the work would get stuck. Hanumant liked to go to the building site, and I accompanied him. Maybe, one day, another bridge will be made and Hanumant would supervise the construction, I thought, looking at Hanumant, who was gazing at the bridge.

'Come, friend,' I said, 'how long will you stare at the bridge? This is an ordinary bridge, yours will be something else. Yes! Come now, I'm feeling thirsty. Let's go and have a cold drink at one of the shops in the market. Ma has given me money to get lemonade.'

We then spotted Hanumant's father—head of the workers. We greeted each other and I asked him to tell Papa that we were going to the market and then back to our house.

As we walked into the town it looked like many people knew Hanumant. All along the way, he kept greeting many kakas and mamas with a namaste. Because of him, some also recognized me. Our country is wonderful—uncles, aunts, brothers and sisters are all acquired while walking on the road, as if we all belong to one big family! When I later said

In Search of a River

this to Papa, he said that this used to be our culture, and that it is rather sad that we were forgetting it now.

At the cold drink shop, Hanumant stood outside and called, 'Kaka, we want two cold drinks.'

The shop owner spoke from inside. 'Since when have you become a babu?'

'It's not for me. With me is the Engineer Babu's son; he wants it,' Hanumant replied with a smile. He then turned towards me and said that we should go inside.

Inside the shop, there were benches where people were sitting, eating and drinking. We also sat on a bench. The shop owner came to us and said, 'I have met the Engineer Babu. When did you come? This is your first visit to my shop. It makes me very happy.'

'My name is Bharat, please call me by my name.' I greeted him with a namaste.

'Fine, I will call you Bharat bhaiya.' He smiled and asked, 'What will you drink?'

'Any drink, which is cold—if you have lemonade, please give me that. I am very thirsty. We walked all the way to the bridge and then to the town,' I said.

'Can I get you something to eat? You have come to our shop for the first time.'

'No, thank you. Ma is waiting at home for me with food.'

'What will you have?' he asked Hanumant.

'Give me anything ... you don't have to ask *me*,' he replied.

After a few minutes, two cold bottles of lemonade and four gulab jamuns were in front of us. Hanumant pushed one plate towards me and said, 'Eat one, you will love it! They are fresh. Badri Kaka's gulab jamuns are famous.'

Seeing them, I suddenly felt hungry. I picked one up and popped it into my mouth. They really were delicious! Badri Kaka left us and we sat back, drinking our lemonade and looking around. We noticed two men, who had finished drinking their tea, get up and leave the shop. One of them had a cigarette in his hand, which he threw on the ground and crushed with his shoe. As he walked away, Hanumant leapt from the bench and picked up the cigarette stub.

'See!' he said in an excited whisper. 'This is exactly like the one we found on the hill. You will not find anyone from around here who smokes cigarettes like this.'

'Since when have you started jasoosi, master spy?' I asked humorously, not fully understanding his interest in the cigarette or the men.

'I'm sure they are strangers, but I must find out more. I will ask Badri Kaka. He knows all the people who live here and also those who come from outside,' he said, rushing back into the shop.

He returned soon and said, 'As I had thought—the two men are not from here. They arrived three days ago.'

In Search of a River

'What does it matter. Many people from outside must come here,' I said. Hanumant was frowning as he spoke. 'These people are new to this area, and they go up the hill—why? Hardly anyone from outside goes to the hill. I must go home and tell Baba about this. Do you think they have heard the story about the hill and the king's treasure, and they went to hunt for it?'

He sounded so worried about the two strangers that it also alarmed me.

'Let's go home,' I said and got up. When we went to pay, Badri Kaka wouldn't take any money for the gulab jamuns. He charged only for the cold drinks, and even that he accepted very reluctantly.

On our way back home, Hanumant was quiet, deep in thought. Before entering my home, I shook him and said, 'Don't think any more, Mr Detective. You will find many cigarettes like these elsewhere. Go home and rest, and give my pranam to Baba.'

I noticed that he was not smiling. He walked away swiftly as he was headed towards his village.

Seven

At dinner, I told Papa about the cigarette butts—the same kind Hanumant and I had seen on the hillside and then again outside the sweetshop, being tossed by the two men that day. Upon hearing this, he was amused and asked, 'Does Master Hanumant want to become a detective?'

In turn, I asked, 'Papa, how many years does one have to study to become an engineer, and where can one study?'

'Who wants to study, you?' he asked and looked teasingly at Ma, knowing that the very thought of my becoming an engineer would upset her.

'No, not for me. I am asking for Hanumant,' I said quickly. Ma looked relieved and Papa said, 'He will have to work very hard. First, he will have to pass the tenth class with a good division. Then, in classes eleven and

In Search of a River

twelve, he will have to study science subjects at a high level. Then, five years in an engineering college—it is a long road for him.'

I too added up the years. He was now in his sixth year of school—four years, then two, and then, five—that meant another eleven years! It did seem like a long road to achievement.

Papa said, 'Actually, thinking about it, when he passes out from the local school, he will need additional help to cope with the tough subjects. He will have to work hard—with or without help—because one has to work hard to get what one wants. One has to climb the stairs to reach the top. Without climbing, you cannot reach the top!'

'Can you help him, Papa?' I asked earnestly.

'I can certainly try. He is a clever boy. I will talk to Bisu Sardar—his father, and also meet with the headmaster of his school. But I may be here today, and tomorrow I may be somewhere far away. The hard work has to be done by him.'

I planned to tell Hanumant all that Papa had told me. We had known each other for a short time, but I understood that we were growing up under very different circumstances. He lacked my advantages—education in such a small village school was limited, and there was no one at home to help him. But I was sure, from the little I had seen of him, that although the road may be long and difficult, he was not one to give up and accept failure or defeat. Nothing would stop him from reaching his destination.

When I went to bed that night, I once again thought of the two men and Hanumant's concerns about their presence in the hill. It started worrying me too, and I could barely sleep.

We met early the next morning. He seemed to be bursting with some new information, and insisted, 'You come and talk to Baba.'

'I thought about it a lot last night,' I replied. Then, I suggested, 'Why don't we talk to Misir Kaka? He has been living here for a long time and must know a great deal about the people in this area.'

'All right,' Hanumant said, 'but you go ahead—because when he sees me, he picks up his stick!'

I found Misir Kaka sitting on a cot under a tree, smoking his hukka. Seeing me, he said, 'Come ... come, Bharat bhaiya! You've remembered me after many days. Where do you wander around these days?'

'Here and there; this is a beautiful place.' I sat down near him.

'But today, your friend, the monkey, is not with you—where is he?' he asked, looking around.

Before I could answer, Hanumant suddenly appeared from wherever he was hiding, and sat close to Misir Kaka's feet.

In Search of a River

Folding his hands in a namaskar, he said, 'Hanumant does pranam to you!'

I was surprised and just stared at him. It seemed to me that Hanumant's talents might be wasted in becoming an engineer. He would make a very good actor!

Misir Kaka jumped up, covered his ears and said, 'Ram, Ram! This boy is really troublesome!'

It made me laugh and ask, 'So many people who are named Ram or Krishna are naughty and are scolded by their parents. Why do you get so upset?'

Misir Kaka said very solemnly, 'Bhaiya, Bajrangbali is our God. How can we insult him by saying his name?'

What an effect this had on Hanumant! With folded hands and very politely, he said, 'I will never upset you again, Misir Kaka. Just forgive me, this time.'

I was amazed by Hanumant's tone. How could he change his mischievous way of speaking and acting so quickly? Misir Kaka recovered from his surprise, relaxed and then said, 'You don't have to act like this any more. Tell me, why are you doing all this drama? What is it you both want from me?' Turning towards me, he said, 'Bharat bhaiya, you are both making me very curious. What is it that I can do for you?'

Now we had to tell him the purpose of our visit. I said, 'Misir Kaka, we went up the hill and found a few cigarette butts there ... see these?' and I showed him the cigarette ends.

In Search of a River

'Don't keep them in your hands, these are dirty! Why are they of interest to you? Are you thinking of smoking? If you put them in your mouth, I will tell Engineer Babu,' he said, becoming quite upset.

'Oh, Misir Kaka, how can you think that! Of course, we are not going to do that. We want to know if you have seen anyone smoking these cigarettes.' I tried to calm him down.

'So many people smoke cigarettes, who can I name?' he replied.

'Please look at these—don't they look very different from what we see locally? Do you think these are videshi?' I asked and held the cigarette stubs up to him.

He bent down, examined them, then said, 'Yes, you may be right. They do look different from what I usually see.'

'If you see anyone smoking cigarettes like these will you please tell us, Misir Kaka?' I requested.

He was startled and asked, 'Why?'

I was not ready for this question. Explaining our reason meant that we would have to tell him *everything*. After thinking about it, I said, 'We are playing a game. If it is a local person, then I will be right, while Hanumant says that the smoker is a videshi.' I thought I had given a very good reason, but Misir Kaka didn't seem to believe me.

He looked at us suspiciously for a moment, then nodded and said, 'All right, if I see anyone, I will tell you, but remember you are not to smoke a bidi or a cigarette. If you do, I will punish you both.'

We left Misir Kaka's garden and went to see Hanumant's Baba. When we told him about the cigarettes and the two foreigners, he became thoughtful and his answer was unexpected. 'It is very sad that so many of our people have lost all love and respect for our own tribe. Their love for money controls them. I have heard stories about outsiders who come here, and give our tribal people money to take away our old treasures. So many idols from our old temples have disappeared like this. I don't know what they do with them. My sorrow is that our own children help them in these evil deeds. It may be that word has spread about the missing throne and crown of the king. And now outsiders are wandering around, looking for them.'

Baba pointed at Hanumant and said, 'This boy is small and childish. I don't want you two to get into any trouble. I am afraid of that. I don't want you to go to the hill.' Baba said seriously, trying to warn us.

Hearing Baba's words I felt that he truly feared for our safety from the greedy and dangerous people who might be around. That was the reason he did not want us to go near the hill. I wanted to obey him, but the hill was *our* place, where we searched for the truth of many mysteries. Unless we looked around there, we would not find any clues. As

In Search of a River

we left Baba, I told Hanumant about the rivers that flow underground and all that Papa had told me. He listened very attentively, became very excited, and said, 'It really seems that what Baba says about the river going underground could be true.'

'But your river was flowing on the ground. Why would it go underground?' I asked.

'That is what we have to discover. If it is true, then I think we may find the throne and the crown too.' Now Hanumant was really excited. I understood that if he could bring the river back, it would make him the happiest person on earth. And, if I could help him in this search, I would also be very happy. Preoccupied with all these thoughts, we walked to my home. Hanumant's great ambition was to build a bridge on the lost river. But before that, I had to return to school after my holidays. Over the past few days, I had seen and learnt so much about things that my school would never teach—I had learnt about a strange snake, vanished rivers, lost treasures, and now, most recently from Baba, about greedy outsiders stripping tribal people of their ancient valuables, including temple idols. However, it was difficult to know how to connect the dots. I had much more to learn and understand.

It was clear that in the remaining days we would have to focus on solving these mysteries. However, in the middle of these unsolved mysteries, my bow and arrow lessons were forgotten altogether. In any case, my teacher was now more interested in detective work rather than teaching me.

Eight

It rained heavily for the next two days. Ma stopped my going outside and wandering about. If I got wet in the rain and became ill, what would happen to me in this jungle?

When Papa heard this, he couldn't help laughing and said, 'Kamla, you can think of so many dangers and problems. I never stop being surprised! He is a human child, not made of wax. If he falls ill, we will get a doctor to treat him. This is a small town, why do you think that this is a jungle? I just don't understand! Think about the problems I have to face on the building site. You know how worried we are about the rains affecting the work. Believe me, they won't harm Bharat.'

Ma looked annoyed as she went towards the kitchen.

Papa smiled, but we both knew that I wouldn't be able to move about freely any time soon.

On the third day of my imprisonment at home, it didn't rain in the morning, but in the afternoon, there was a heavy storm. The wind was so strong that the trees around us looked as if they would fly away. Branches broke and came tumbling down. I had no choice but to stay indoors and read.

I soon grew fed up of just sitting, and went upstairs to look at the wind-tossed trees from my window. I was shocked to see Hanumant rushing towards our house. Earlier, he used to sit on the boundary wall and wait for me. When I asked him why he stayed at a distance, he told me that he was afraid of Bahuji, my mother. 'Why are you afraid of her?' I had asked, and he said that she might complain to his father and stop him from coming. It seemed like everyone was afraid of my mother.

Therefore, I was surprised to see Hanumant, coming straight towards our front door through the storm. What could have made him forget his fear? I rushed towards the door, but Ma was there before me. She was astonished to see him.

Hanumant politely greeted her with a namaste. Then, hesitatingly, he asked, 'Bahuji, is Bharat home?'

Before she could reply, I said from behind her, 'Oh, where were you, Hanumant? For the past two days, I couldn't

In Search of a River

even see your tail!' Then I grabbed his hand and pulled him inside. 'Come, come inside. This is the first time that you have come to our house.'

After being stuck inside the house for the past few days, I was happy to see him and very curious about why he had come to our house in the middle of a storm.

I took him to my room, and once we were inside, Hanumant looked around to see if there was anyone else there. Seeing no one, he said in a low voice, 'I have found the way to go inside the hill.'

'What!' I said, completely stunned.

'Yes, Bharat. For the past two days, because it was raining, I could not come this way, nor could I go towards the hill. It stopped raining this morning, so I went to the hill. Then came the storm. I was sitting near the wall by the old tree, and the tree was uprooted and it fell! I was afraid and ran to the other side. When the storm stopped, I went back to the old tree. The roots were all up in the air and I saw.... Bharat, I am telling you the truth ... that at the very spot where the tree stood tall before being felled, there was now an opening and a passage! To go underground, like a tunnel.' Saying this, he started breathing very deeply.

I could scarcely believe him. 'Hanumant, you are too obsessed and mad about the underground river and you have started seeing underground passages everywhere,' I told him,

In Search of a River

trying to explain away something that seemed too fantastic.

'No. I am telling you the truth. In fact, there was a big stone covering the hole in the ground. The tree's roots had covered the stone. When the tree fell, the roots must have knocked the stone away. Bharat, I really think this is an opening and passage to go under the hill.'

He was so insistent that I started to believe him a little. I asked, 'The passage goes which way?'

'I couldn't see that properly, but I felt cold air from below the earth,' he said excitedly and his eyes were shining. 'I have covered the hole with branches and stones. Tomorrow morning, we must go and see it.'

Now I too felt impatient and eager to see it. But Hanumant was right—we would have to wait till tomorrow. Even if we rushed towards the hill, it would be dark by the time we got there and we would not be able to see anything properly.

'Have you told anyone else?' I asked.

'No. I thought I should tell Baba, but then I wanted to tell you first and came straight here.'

I was filled with curiosity. So many questions whirled in my head. Would we be able to find the throne and the king's crown? Would we be able to bring the river of Hanumant's imagination all the way—from underground to our earth—where he would then make a wonderful bridge? Was this the beginning of the wonders of his imagination?

Hanumant's eyes sparkled with light, as though reflecting this imagined future. But I suddenly felt anxious. 'If someone else finds the hole, then?'

'No. No one will be able to see it. I have covered it properly ...' He paused.

'What?' I urged.

'Don't laugh. I didn't want to tell you before, but I have asked my nag devata to look after it. He will guard it, I am sure,' he said with great faith.

Hearing this, I felt like laughing, but I did not laugh. I had started to understand his way of thinking and I respected his beliefs; they were based on old ideas and customs. My father said that these customs and beliefs are very important to tribal life. We cannot take them away, only they can change them.

I asked Hanumant, 'Did you meet the nag devata?'

'No, I did not see him, but he also hears my thoughts, wherever he may be. I'm sure he is guarding the hole. But we must go early tomorrow morning. Once it stops raining, other people will go there to collect wood. Everyone knows that a lot of branches and trees have fallen due to the storm.'

What Hanumant said was right, whatever we did, it had to be soon. But I wondered if we would be able to do what was necessary all by ourselves. However, if others helped us, then it would no longer be *our* search. He may have been

In Search of a River

thinking about this as well. So, I said, 'That is best, don't tell anyone else. If it does not rain, then we will go early in the morning and decide what to do next.'

'What are you two planning?' Ma asked suddenly, entering the room. She had a plate with sweets and two glasses of sherbet in her hand. Giving the sweets to Hanumant, she said, 'Eat these. I have made them. Hanuman ji likes them and you will like them too. They are laddoos.' She smiled affectionately.

We were a little nervous when she entered, but her smile allayed my anxiety. Still, we had to hide our plans from her. We could not tell her that we were planning to go up the hill tomorrow. Nothing could delay us, otherwise people would get to the fallen tree before us and ruin Hanumant's discovery. I made a sign to ensure Hanumant did not say anything but he had realized the need for secrecy himself, and quietly started to eat the *laddoos*. Only after Ma left the room did we make some plans for the next day.

It was such an important day for our search, brimming with unknowns, with much for us to discover. If we were lucky, it could be the final day of our search!

Nine

Next morning, I got up very early. In fact, I was wide awake for almost half the night and when I finally fell asleep, in my dreams I saw the crown, the throne and with them, Hanumant's nag devata. I was worried about the rain; if the rain did not stop, I was afraid that Ma would prevent me from going out. In any case, after Hanumant's visit yesterday, she was already a little suspicious about our plans.

Opening my eyes in the morning, and seeing the sun shining bright, I was so happy that it is impossible to express it!

One problem solved, now Ma would surely agree to our going out.

I got ready quickly and had started to eat breakfast when Hanumant arrived. Most probably, he had been unable to

In Search of a River

sleep last night—just like me. Maybe he had been guarding the hilltop all night!

Seeing him, Ma asked, 'Now where are you planning to go? Yesterday, there was such a storm! God only knows how many trees have fallen everywhere.'

'What does it matter. We're not going to pick up fallen trees! I have been sitting at home since two or three days, and I'm fed up—going out will be a change for us,' I said, trying to stop her from worrying.

'I'd like to know what you are planning. Seeing your friend yesterday has made me suspicious about today's outing. Your father has no worries ... he goes away in the morning, putting on his cap, to supervise the bridge. All the worrying is left to me,' she grumbled, going to the kitchen. I went after her, telling her, as calmly as I could, that we would be very careful, that I loved her, that I understood her worries, and she eventually agreed to let me step outside.

Once outside, Hanumant and I raced towards the hill. On our way, we had to lift quite a number of fallen branches and bricks from our path. Some people, mostly women and children from the nearby village, had already come to collect the wood. But they were downhill.

Seeing them, Hanumant quickened his pace. 'I'm worried about them. If they go up the hill and start collecting the broken branches there, they may also pick up the branches

I had piled on top of the hole. Let's go quickly.'

We decided to climb the hill from a side path, so the people below couldn't see our ascent. Hanumant was climbing very fast, leaping along. I couldn't keep up with him and was climbing slowly behind him.

When we reached the hilltop, we looked around anxiously, relieved to see that no one had reached before us. Studying the ground, Hanumant asked me, 'Bharat, have you seen any burnt cigarette ends anywhere?'

'Cigarettes?' I asked in surprise. Then I remembered the two people we had seen at the tea stall and our conversations about them with Misir Kaka and Baba. 'Why will they come here? They do not want broken branches for firewood,' I said, smiling.

'They may not need wood, but they may probably be searching for something else,' Hanumant said ominously. We had reached the big tree on the hill's peak. The broken walls of the old palace were still standing, but the tree had fallen and was lying on its side. Curiously, I tried to go near the hole, but then I suddenly remembered Hanumant's nag devata and remained where I was.

Up ahead, Hanumant turned and asked, 'What happened? Why are you standing there?'

'Where is your nag devata?' I asked cautiously, glancing around.

In Search of a River

Hanumant grinned. 'He may be somewhere near about. Don't be afraid. Come and see this.'

He had faith in his snake god, but I walked very warily. The god may be Hanumant's friend, but I was afraid the moment his name was mentioned. Seeing him once had been enough for me!

Hanumant pointed to a pile of stones and branches. 'I put them there to cover the hole, and they are still there.' In fact, I saw quite a number of branches and leaves had fallen in a pile around them. Looking around to make sure there was no one else nearby, we started clearing the spot. We worked rapidly to remove the stones, and all the while Hanumant kept looking left and right.

When all the stones were cleared, we found a square hole in front of us. It looked very deep, like the mouth of an underground passage. We bent low to peer inside, but we couldn't see anything properly. I had a torch, which I had brought from the house, and even a candle and a matchbox, which Hanumant had asked me to bring. If Ma had known about this, there would have been great trouble, so these had to be hidden! We switched on the torch, and shone it into the hole, but still couldn't see much inside. We could only make out that there was an underground passage, and that it seemed quite long.

Taking the torch from me, Hanumant said, 'I'll go first.

In Search of a River

You stay up here. I'll keep calling you so that you know that I am all right. I want to find out where this passage goes and how long it is.'

'No, you must not go alone!' I stopped him. 'Let's go back and get a few more people from the village.' Seeing that dark passage underground, I was afraid.

'See, Bharat, if we get other people here, they will make us go back home, and then, they will go in themselves. Don't be frightened, I will not go far. You will be able to see with the torchlight. And nag devata is somewhere near about—he will look after me.' He said this part with a wide smile, most probably to tease me.

'Now, I am even more afraid! How can you think of leaving me alone here with your nag devata!'

But Hanumant just said 'No. I will go and come soon' and jumped inside the hole.

I leaned over the edge and from the moving light of the torch I could tell that he was trying to see all around and along the passage.

I shouted, 'Can you see anything?'

'This passage is a way to the underground, I think. I will explore it … but don't worry, I won't go far.' Having said this, he went further away. I could not stop him. He seemed full of courage, and I wondered if it had arisen from the hope of finding the throne and the crown. His voice became very faint and my fear grew. If something happened to him, what would his Baba and mother do? My Papa would also be furious with me. I suddenly found myself praying, 'nag devata, please look after him', and repeating the names of all the gods and goddesses I could remember.

Suddenly, I heard his voice.

'Bharat, come! The passage is quite good.'

With a 'Jai Bajrangbali', I also jumped into the passage. I briefly thought: if Hanuman ji is calling, why should there be any fear? Maybe it's true that if we believe and pray then we become stronger.

I entered the underground passage and started crawling forward. Hanumant called out, 'Come slowly towards me. I am shining the torchlight towards you.'

The passage was not very dark. I kept moving ahead slowly, as the passage was not very broad and I was squeezed between the walls. Suddenly, the light became very bright and Hanumant's voice rang out loud.

'There is a sharp turn in front,' he said, and abruptly, the passage turned and I found myself in front of Hanumant. Seeing him safe and sound, I was happier than I would have been to find any treasure. Taking his hand in my hands, I asked, 'Where are we, in heaven or under the earth?'

'We are now in a room inside the hill,' he said and moved the torchlight. I also saw that we were in an open

In Search of a River

space—a small room.

'Now what?' I asked uncertainly.

'Take the candle from your pocket and light it. Only then we will be able to see properly. Why are you looking at me like that? Am I a ghost!' he said, laughing.

I took out the matchbox and reluctantly lit the candle, praying that the air around me would not explode because of some trapped gas! The wick lit up brightly and thankfully nothing else happened. Looking around I saw that the walls around us seemed to be made of heavy stone slabs. Hanumant was also looking around and as we were moving away from one of the walls, we suddenly felt a gust of air coming from a gap between two stones.

'This must be the way to the mountain,' said Hanumant excitedly. 'Come let's try and move these stones.' We pushed hard against the two large stones but nothing moved.

The flame from the candle flickered and Hanumant said, 'We need some help to get to the mountain. Maybe you should go down the hill to my village and tell my Baba and mother to bring some people here.'

'And leave you alone here? I can't do that!' I said, worried.

'Don't worry about me, just go.' Hanumant's eyes gleamed brightly in the candlelight. 'Nag devata will look after me!'

Ten

I ran down the hill.

Hanumant was inside the passage but he had asked me to go to his village and tell his Baba everything. My father was too far away, at work on the bridge.

I trammelled down the hill as quickly as possible. I was afraid of leaving Hanumant alone, but there was no other way I could inform the others about what I had seen. Reaching down to the dry bank, I thought about the river that had gone underground. Would we find out if the river had gone underground? Is it possible that we would bring the river back after we had found it?

Baba was sitting outside his house. I ran up to him and sat down; it took me some time to catch my breath and calm down. He looked at me in surprise. Maybe he couldn't

In Search of a River

recognize me because his eyesight wasn't good. So, I told him my name and all that had happened. I didn't think he understood what I said. He called for Hanumant's mother and when she came out of the house, he said something to her, pointing at me. It was getting late and Hanumant was alone on the hill.

I took his hand, and lifting him up I said, 'Baba, you come with me to the hill. Hanumant is all alone. Send someone to the bridge to inform my Papa ji. He should also come to the hill with a few people. Do you understand? We have found the way to go under the hill.'

I think Hanumant's mother understood some of my message. She went to the other homes and started calling people by their names. Few people were at home at such an hour, but still, three or four of them came out. She told one of them something, which made him look at me, and then he went towards the bridge.

Hanumant's mother, his Baba, two of the village men and I moved towards the hill.

Baba was not able to walk fast, so all of us were moving slowly. Seeing my worried face, Hanumant's mother told the two men to go up faster. I kept thinking that it had been almost an hour since I had left Hanumant on the hill. What must he be facing and doing all by himself? It would take us at least half an hour more to reach the top.

The man who had gone to call my father would not be able to come soon either. I kept adding up the minutes and hours it would take to reach the top.

To climb up the mountain path, Baba needed two people to help him. When we finally reached the top, I looked at Hanumant's mother. She understood my feelings and made a sign for me to go on ahead.

Two others from the village had already reached the top. She asked them to stay with me and the three of us went towards the broken walls of the palace. I hoped to see Hanumant safe, sitting near the fallen tree and the hole. I also hoped that on hearing our voices he would come and meet us. But he was nowhere to be seen. The two villagers with me stared at the hole by the tree in surprise.

I began looking around for Hanumant. I saw his mother and his Baba approaching us and shook my head, indicating that I couldn't see Hanumant. Thinking that he might still be in the underground passage, I shouted into the hole, 'Hanumant, where are you?' but there was no reply, except for my voice echoing back.

Our small group looked at each other with dismay, and called out his name many times, but he never replied. I went closer to the edge of the hole to look as far as I could, and then, I saw a burnt cigarette end. I picked it up with trembling hands and a growing dread.

In Search of a River

I knew then that my fear and suspicions had been right—it was the same kind of cigarette butt that we had seen before. Earlier that morning, it had not been there. Someone had thrown it there after I left. Speaking to Hanumant's mother and his Baba, I said 'He is in danger, I am sure of this.'

His mother's face twisted with fear.

'I will go inside and look,' I said.

This time, she made a sign, asking me not to go.

'Please ask one of the men to come down with me. The others will stay with you. We must not delay.' Saying this, I jumped into the hole. I felt another person jump in after me. Then both of us pushed ahead.

I was afraid. What would happen if the strange men were inside? But we had to find Hanumant, no matter how dangerous it was. I called him two, three times, but did not get a reply. Someone handed me a torch. I switched it on. The space in front of us lit up and I almost fainted in fear.

There, in a far corner, was Hanumant—his feet and hands bound with rope and his mouth gagged with a cloth so he could not make any sound. Once he saw us coming towards him, he raised his head. There was still fear in his eyes. I untied the cloth covering his mouth. The moment the cloth was undone, he said, 'Be careful. Those three cigarette smokers are here and have gone inside the hill.'

In Search of a River

He pointed towards his left. When I shone the torch that way, I was surprised to see a small opening, like an open window—a gush of cool air was blowing in from there. It was at the exact point where we had tried to shift the stones before. We had not looked at that side so far since we were in a hurry to untie Hanumant's hands and feet.

I noticed a stone that had been moved to make the opening. This meant that there was a way to go into the hill from here. I saw a number of steps descending into the dark. But where were those people? We could not hear any sound from down there.

I asked Hanumant, 'How did they tie you up?'

His legs and hands now untied, he was rubbing and flexing them. He replied that most probably they had followed us when we went into the underground passage, or maybe when we climbed the hill. They had stayed hidden till I went to call Baba, and when he was alone, they caught him.

'They took me to the tunnel and tied my mouth so that I could not shout. Then they lit a mashaal that they had brought with them. They loosened the stone with iron rods and moved it.'

'Did they know I would come back with more people?' I asked.

'They heard everything. One of them lives nearby and he knew that it would take you more than an hour to get back from the village, because there won't be people in the village at this time.'

'Where are they?' I asked, looking around. By now, a few more people had reached the small room where we were. Hanumant's mother was among them. Upon seeing her son, tears rolled down her eyes. She had been controlling herself all this while. I too felt stronger, thinking Papa and others would soon be here with Hanumant's father.

'Where have those three gone?' I asked again.

'They have gone down,' Hanumant replied.

'Is there another way inside the hill?'

'Until we go down and look around, we won't be able to find any other way,' he said.

We could now hear lots of voices above us. It seemed that many others had come up the hill. I heard Papa's voice. 'Where are Bharat and Hanumant?' He was preparing to come down.

'Papa, please stay there. We are coming up,' I said. There was not enough space for more people down here, especially for a tall person like Papa. It was better for us to go up. If they came down, they would have to come one by one; the earlier group had made the passage narrower by pushing the stone near the mouth of the opening.

Hanumant went up first. I was behind him. Seeing him, those standing on the hill started clapping in joy. Papa and

In Search of a River

Bisu Sardar put their hands on Hanumant's shoulder and gave him their blessings. Then Papa asked him what had happened.

Hanumant looked at me and then, slowly, told them all that had happened while we were looking for the river. Some of it Papa already knew from the villagers. Hanumant described how the three men had caught hold of him and taken him to a corner inside the cave.

'They did not ask you anything?' Papa said.

'They asked me how long Bharat would take to come back. I tried to frighten them by saying that he would be back in half an hour with you all.'

'Then?'

'With them was one man who seemed local. He said that this boy is telling lies. No one will be able to come before one and a half hours.'

'Did you recognize him? Have you seen him before?'

Hanumant shook his head.

Then Papa asked, 'How did they remove the stone?'

'They lit a mashaal, took it near the stone and pushed it many times. Then they tried to move the stone with a big, thick stick. It got loose after some time.'

'When they went down, did they say something to you?'

'No, they were speaking among themselves, saying, "If the crown is here, it will not take us long to find it. We will go away before the people from the village can find us."'

Now, Papa looked at Bisu Sardar and said, 'They must have come in a car. But where are they now? Are they still inside? I think we should go down—don't you think so?' He had posed this question to everyone around. They all agreed with him.

So, all of us were prepared to go underground. Four big mashaals were arranged. First, we had to reach the room through the tunnel. This was dangerous. We did not know if the men were hiding there. The first person to enter would have to face the danger alone. Hanumant's father, Bisu Sardar, insisted on going in first. Four others carrying a lit mashaal each would follow him.

Everyone was keen to go down, especially Hanumant and I. We would finally discover what we had been looking for all along.

Eleven

Hanumant's father was the first to go ahead into the tunnel. Four men went in after him with flaming mashaals. My Papa tied a rope around his waist and asked Bisu Sardar to shake it if he found the underground tunnel empty. If the rope did not shake, we would know that those people had returned to the stone cave.

After some time, the rope shook.

We lit the lamp and started going down. The rope shook again.

By now, quite a lot of people had reached the top of the hill and were standing around the entrance of the tunnel. Papa asked four or five of them to stay with Baba.

When Hanumant and I reached the cave, the people ahead of us were going down the stone steps with their mashaals.

We followed them. There were about thirty stone steps along the wall on the hillside. Papa also had a torch in his hand. It was a wonderful, adventurous and mysterious scene. We did not know how far below we were; it seemed like these steps were leading us into the depths of the earth. The stone walls around us were shining, illuminated by the light from the flaming mashaals, as if they had flecks of silver and gold.

As we descended the last few steps, we suddenly saw a pool of water below.

We had reached the bottom. On the right was dry ground and what we saw in front of us was stunning. It was like a scene set on a stage. The ones holding the mashaal stood stock still and we too stopped dead on the last step.

Ahead of us, on the right, was a big stone chair. It had four stone legs, carved intricately, on which rested a beautiful square-shaped stone. On it was placed an object that was clearly a crown.

The crown was a little dark but it was studded with colourful stones, gleaming in the light of the mashaals. The light, as it touched the water in the pond, also had another remarkable effect—it moved with the water. The rippling, moving light fell on three people who were standing near the stone wall. They were still, almost frozen—like statues. We were stunned as well and stood motionless.

Then my eyes went towards their legs—I closed my eyes

In Search of a River

and opened them again. What I had seen was true. There were two snakes right in front of them, with their hoods spread wide. The others had seen the snakes and couldn't move. No one had the courage to go ahead.

Suddenly, Hanumant, who was in front of me, said, 'These are the nag devatas.'

Before anyone could stop him, pushing the others aside, he stepped down the last step. His father tried to stop him, but failed; Hanumant evaded his hand. Hanumant moved slowly towards the pond and the throne. Seeing him, a snake slid towards him. Hanumant folded his hands and said something, which we could not hear—it was as though we were spectators watching a play being enacted in front of us.

Slowly, the snake started crawling towards Hanumant. I closed my eyes, fearful that the snake would bite him. I did not want to see it. When I opened my eyes, the snake had moved past my friend and was actually headed towards the throne. I noticed then—a big hole in the wall behind the throne. I watched as the snake slipped into it. The three men were also watching it. They seemed to be completely frozen with fear, unable to stir.

Hanumant then walked calmly away from the other snake, which had remained near their feet. Hanumant went ahead and lifted the crown with both his hands. Holding the crown, he turned and came towards us. His expression

In Search of a River

was radiant, as if he had won a great victory!

A scene like this seemed utterly fantastic. While we stood, still like stone figures Hanumant, with the crown in his hands, went up straight towards his father. As he came towards us, it seemed as if we had woken up from a dream.

Everyone started talking excitedly. It was then that I saw the snake guarding the three men also turn and disappear through the hole like the other snake. But the three men still remained in the same spot. It seemed like they had lost the power to move.

I went towards Hanumant who was standing like a victorious soldier between his father and my Papa. I touched his shoulder and we looked at each other with immense joy. This was the reward of our joint search. But the spirit of the search was Hanumant's, and so was the courage and strength it required.

I still had not fully grasped that we had found the king's lost throne and crown. Neither the king nor his sons were there. This discovery had great meaning for the tribal people. This was a part of their history, and they now had actual proof of it. It would be with them always.

What happened afterwards is difficult to say. There was a lot of shouting and jumping. A group of five or six people went after those three men and caught them. They were gradually waking up, coming back from their almost unconscious state.

They were truly happy that they were saved from the wrath of the snakes. At least they would live, even if they had to go to prison.

After being captured, they were brought outside. Papa studied the pond and the area around before leaving. Outside, a few policemen had arrived at the hilltop. The police were on guard around the hill. Then, we all came down the hill in a joyful procession.

The next day, Papa and some district officials went back to the hill and examined the pond. To find out where the water originated and where it went required a lot of careful study. However, after much ado they found the lost river, and also discovered the reason for its disappearance. As Papa explained, there was a way for the river to flow out through the wall behind the throne, which had become blocked by stones. The stones had been put there on purpose in such a way that no one could find them from outside. The king was himself a very clever engineer! Maybe the river did go underground in anger—the king's anger!

A few days after this discovery, the stones were removed from the opening. At first, water was only trickling out, but soon it began to spurt, and the river began to fill up. It was so satisfying to see the river, Hanumant's river, no longer underground in anger. One day, his beautiful bridge would come up on it and his wish would be fulfilled.

In Search of a River

My holiday had also come to an end. I had to say goodbye to my friend Hanumant. The district head came and told us that Hanumant would be admitted to the army school. He could study there and then join an engineering college. He would be given all the help he needed to excel at his studies.

Being aware of Hanumant's capacity to work hard, I was totally convinced about his ability to acquire knowledge and fulfil his ambition. No obstructions and difficulties would be able to stop him, and we would always be friends. We continued to stay in touch through letters. I told him that the day he would finish building his bridge, he should inform me, irrespective of where I would be. After the construction, both of us would walk on the new bridge. We were friends, and our friendship was forever.

My search with Hanumant had shown me a path as well.

I wanted to study the historical roots of human beings and share my learnings with everyone. By now you must have realized that I want to be an archaeologist, which in Hindi is known as Puratatva Vaigyanic.

When my mother heard this, she was very upset and angry. She said, 'This is worse than being an engineer, you will spend your whole life in jungles, amongst ruins.'

Papa heard this and burst into laughter.